AUTHOR'S NOTE

This is a creative partnership between you and me. For this book to be complete, I invite you to add a piece of yourself to each and every page.

You are the creator of what is to become a permanent record of who you are, how you see yourself and how you see the world at this moment in time.

Have fun, my fellow artists!

Dedicated to my mom...

Because of you, I get to be me.

Appreciation starts with **A**
And is a feeling light and gay.
It makes a heart just fill with joy
Inside most every girl and boy.

It starts out with a "Thank You" for
The miracles of life galore.
And surely does this gratitude
Just put you in the finest mood.

Appreciate a sunny day,
Or just the view along the way.
Be thankful for the deep blue sea,
Appreciate a fuzzy bee.

Let's take a moment here and now
And make ourselves a simple vow,
By promising we'll live and play,
Appreciating every day.

THANK YOU for reading this. Now it's your turn.
What do you **appreciate**?

The **beauty** of the letter **B**
Is such a great delight,
Because you see it everywhere,
It's really quite a sight.

You see it in the plants that grow,
You see it in the sky.
You see it in the grandest lakes
Or in the smallest fly.

You'll also find it deep inside
Where thoughts are sweet and kind,
The part of you that feels love
With both your heart and mind.

So full of **beauty** life can be
So pleasing to the eye.
That it will make you stop and stare
As puffy clouds float by.

We all are born so **beautiful**,
Yet each in our own way.
And that's the **beauty** of this gift
That's shaped in every way.

It's clear that **caring** starts with **C**,
And is a trait of you and me.
It's just a kind and gentle way
Of adding pleasure to your day.

To really **care** about someone
Is often very simply done.
Although it takes some effort to
Show real **care** in all you do.

Now many folks appreciate
The feelings that kind deeds create,
So here's a couple ways to show
That **care** is something that you know.

One **caring** thing to do today
Is make a friend with whom to play.
Then share your toys with this new friend,
The fun you have just might not end!

Gosh, give your mom or dad a treat,
And clean your room up nice and neat.
Or in your classroom show you **care**
By being extra good in there.

Who or what do you **CARE** about most?

D is for **dreaming** and boy, is this great,
These visions that play in the night!
Now sometimes they're sweet and sometimes
  they're strange,
And sometimes they give us a fright.

But always our **dreams** are held in our minds,
Where all of our thoughts can be found,
And often are helpful in showing us ways
Of keeping our feet on the ground.

To **dream** as you sleep is lovely, for sure,
Yet, **dreaming** awake is the best.
Because you can fill up your mind with high hope,
And fill up your heart with great zest.

And when you're awake and can do what you want,
There's really no limit in sight
To what you can hope for and who you can be
Or how you can make all things right.

Remembering always that **dreams** can come true,
Please **dream** to your heart's full desire.
With eyes open wide or when nestled in bed,
Let your **dreams** burn as wild as fire.

If you could have anything you **DREAMED** of, what would it be?

(Maybe each bubble could have it's own wish-list?)

I'm **eager** to get to the **E** in this book,
Where children are welcome to take a close look
At just what it means to be **eager** about
A thing so, so much that you just want to shout!

Let's say that you're **eager** to take a bike ride,
This means that you're bubbling over inside
Because you can't wait to hop on your bike
And zip right on down the path you so like.

Now me – I'm just **eager** to know about you
And all of your friends and your family, too.
I'm **eager** to know all about everything,
Like the future you wish for and what it will bring.

So as you grow up and your stories unfold,
Be **eager** to ponder these tales you're told
Because to be **eager** about all you do
Is yet one more way to be wonderfully you.

What are you most **EAGER** to see or learn or try?

Now, my good **friend**, we've come to **F**,
A letter near at hand,
That starts a word I've often heard
And found in any land.

Why, I myself have tons of **friends**
Who live both near and far,
And each of them is dear to me,
No matter where they are.

See, **friends** are made most anywhere,
They truly are a gift
That keeps on giving all the time
And makes your spirits lift.

Without our **friends**, our life would be
A lonely place, indeed,
So make yourself a friend today
And watch where this will lead.

Who are three of your best **FRIENDS**?
What are their names and why did you choose them?

Friend's name: _____

Best quality: _____

Friend's name: _____

Best quality: _____

Friend's name: _____

Best quality: _____

I'm so **glad** we're up to **G**,
Since **gladness** is a trait
That makes a smile cross your face.
This feeling is so great!

Now when a face just brightens up,
You know someone is **glad,**
And also know, without a doubt,
This person can't be sad.

Since glad and sad can never show
Together on one face.
The two are very opposite,
But both must have their place.

It's never bad to feel **glad**,
I'm sure you've often heard.
In fact, I think we'll both agree
We're **glad** we found this word!

What makes you just so **GLAD** to be you?

Let's hear it for **humor**, a fun-loving word,
And one that is precious to me.
It starts with an **H** and is usually found
In folks who are brimming with glee.

Now **humor** and laughter – they go hand in hand,
The two come together as one,
Because where there's **humor**, there's always a laugh,
Creating a whole bunch of fun.

I think that the **humor** of making a joke,
Or finding the funniest way
Of telling a story to cheer up your pals
Will laugh many troubles away.

See, **humor** is truly a wonderful word,
And found in all people on earth.
It lightens your load and fills you right up
With all sorts of laughter and mirth.

A good sense of **humor** is truly a way,
To bring out the fun side of you,
Remembering always to keep this in mind
As each day begins fresh and new.

What kind of sense of **HUMOR** do you have?
What do you find funny and how might you make other people laugh?

(Do you know any good jokes?)

Imagine if you will, my friends,
A word that starts with **I**,
And one that captures dreamy thoughts
Where wonderment can fly.

It's called **imagination**, and
It's part of you and me.
It's where your thoughts can jump and play,
And run around quite free.

That part of you that can pretend
And play creatively,
Imagining all sorts of scenes
That only you can see.

A kind of magic in your mind
That everyone can make,
That's always there no matter if
You're sleeping or awake.

Imagination is a gift
That comes from deep within,
And tells us all is possible
And everyone can win.

IMAGINE a perfect world. What would it look like?

(Your artistic possibilites are endless here!)

The letter **J** begins our **Joy**,
And **joy** is in the air.
It's seen in faces old and young,
In people everywhere.

True **joy** is much like happiness,
But with a different shade
Of feelings stemming from the heart
Where joy is always made.

To feel **joy** within yourself,
Just take a look around.
You'll see it lives most anywhere,
In every sight and sound.

Like when the breezes make a tree
Dance **joyfully** along
As Mother Nature plays for you
Her favorite joyful song.

Just watch a dolphin swim with **joy**
Or hear a young bird's cheep.
Seek out the **joy** – it's always there,
And loves to make hearts leap.

What fills you up with **JOY**?

Another special part of you
Begins with letter **K**.
And this is one I promise that
You'll simply love to say.

It's **kooky** that I want to add
This silly part of you,
Cuz every kid should have some fun
In what they say and do.

It's not a fancy word, perhaps,
But still, I think it's neat.
And **kooky** people are *for sure*
The types I like to meet.

I've found that many **kooky** kids
Just love to act like goofs
By playing harmless little tricks
And making silly spoofs.

So call me **kooky** if you like,
But me – I like a kid
Who acts so **kooky**, folks will say,
"My gosh, you've flipped your lid!"

What's something **KOOKY** you can do?

(Kooky faces are always appreciated!)

I surely **love** the letter **L**,
It really is so very swell.
And **love** – sweet **love** - is why we're here,
This part of us that knows no fear.

Why, **love** can conquer anything,
And make you want to dance and sing.
It fills you up with family pride,
And even gives you strength inside.

So, **love** this world we call home,
And **love** the beauty of a poem.
And **love** the smell of evening air,
And **love** the stars that twinkle there.

And **love** the plants and critters, too,
And **love** your folks for all they do.
And don't forget to add your friends
To this long list that never ends!

How do you show your **LOVE** and affection for others?

(A love note or family photos might be nice here)

M is simply **magical**,
Of this, I will attest.
A part of life that many think
Is clearly just the best.

We all can seek the **magic** in
This world that we know.
It may just take a watchful eye
To see this **magic** show.

Now, I once saw a **magic** show
That caught my eye, I'll say,
When walking on a sandy shore
One beautiful spring day.

The sun was setting lazily,
Behind the ocean blue,
When suddenly, it flashed at me
A beautiful green hue.

So striking was that ray of light,
It took my breath away,
Because the sun had treated me
To my own **magic** ray.

It's there for you – if you believe
There's **magic** to behold,
So chase your dreams – and rainbows too…
You might find pots of gold!

What do you think is **MAGICAL**?

How **nice** it is to be at **N**
Where **niceness** can be found.
A part of every kid I know –
How charming does that sound?

The **nicest** children in my life
Are favorite friends of mine,
They're always in the greatest mood,
Their smiles really shine.

They let me play with all their toys
And say the **nicest** things.
They often share their lunch with me.
Gosh, even onion rings!

It takes so little to be **nice**,
Yet boy, it feels grand!
So, let's agree that **niceness** rocks
And give **nice** folks a hand!

What is a **NICE** thing you can do for yourself or someone else today?

We've come, my friend, to letter **O**
Where **openness** comes in,
Since **openness** is one more thing
That makes me want to grin.

Now **openness** just simply means
You're always open to
A host of possibilities,
Of which I'll name a few.

Be **open** to new ways to learn
And **open** to advice.
Be **open** to another's view,
(On this, be **open** twice).

Or warmly **open** up your arms
To welcome a new friend,
By **opening** your heart to one
Who needs a heart to mend.

In other words, just **open** up
And let the world in.
There's so much there to see and learn,
Your head will surely spin!

How can you be **OPEN** to trying something new right now?
And what might that look like?

(Here's a great page to put all sorts of words and images.)

How fun it is to be at **P**!
It's quite an active place to be.
Since P starts **pep** – and pep's a word
That packs a punch, or so I've heard.

Now pep begins and ends with P
And in between just has one E,
But though it's small in size, my friend,
Its energy is without end.

So if you'd rather skip than step,
It means you've found yourself some pep.
Or if you're dashing through the park,
Then peppiness has found its mark.

See, peppy people never find
That they are ever left behind,
Because no matter what they do,
Their peppiness just speeds them through.

Yes, pep and peppy simply mean
You're lively as a jumping bean.
Excitement tends to run right through
Most everything you like to do!

How do you put some **PEP** in your step?

(Pictures or stickers of things that make you want to kick up your heels could be fun here!)

Q is kind of kooky
'Cuz the word I picked for Q
Is really quite a mouthful,
But I picked it just for you.

It's **quizzical** that starts with Q,
A word I think you'll find
Describes a way that children can
Expand within their mind.

Now why, you ask, is **quizzical**
A word that you should know?
And I'll say questions such as this,
Tell me you're **quizzical**.

It's all about the questions posed
And wanting to know more,
Like "How do stars dance in the night?"
And "What are insects for?"

It's wondering about the earth
Or how our bodies work,
Or even why the folks we know
Have oh, so many quirks.

So **quiz** yourself and those around,
Just throw some questions out.
Learn more about this thing called "life",
And what it's all about.

What things in your life do you have **QUESTIONS** about?

(Maybe list your questions, then the answers?)

Here's a word that really works,
And starts with letter **R**.
It's longer than the last one learned.
My gosh, we've come so far!

Responsibility, indeed
Is what we'll learn today.
And boy, oh boy, this word is big,
So listen up, I say.

To be **responsible** means this –
You'll do just as you say,
The part of you that follows through
In every sort of way.

It means that when you're nicely asked
To pick up all your toys,
You say you will and then you do,
Like all good girls and boys.

It also means that on your own,
You do your household chores
Or finish all your homework so
You raise your reading scores.

If you do this all by yourself,
Then you're **responsible**.
And all will be so proud of you,
Your heart will swell quite full!

How can you act **RESPONSIBLY**?

I must confess, the letter S
Brings silliness to mind,
Since silly is another part
Of every kid I find.

See, silly people make us laugh,
They like to horse around
And not take life too serious,
At least that's what I've found.

The silly folks I know and love
Just brighten up my day.
They tickle me right to the bone
And take my woes away.

So why not have a little fun
And turn things upside down,
By bringing out your silly side
And acting like a clown?

What do you do when you want to act **SILLY**?

I **trust** we'll find the letter **T**
Exactly where it's meant to be.
It comes right after letter "S"
And just before the "U", no less.

Now, trust is something we can't see,
This quality in you and me.
But is a trait I hold most dear
Because it tells me not to fear.

I trust that every single night
The moon will beam it's lovely light.
And trust that when I sometimes cry,
My mom and dad will ask me why.

I trust that flowers love to bloom
And trust the safety of my room.
I trust what nature teaches me,
And trust that's how it's meant to be.

But most importantly of all,
I trust in children great and small.
So, trust that feeling deep inside
And let it be your trusty guide.

Well, lookie here – we've come to **U**,
The letter for **unique**,
A truly special part of you.
So come, let's take a peak.

To be **unique** means just one thing,
And this is plain to see.
It talks about that part of you
That no one else can be.

When someone is referred to as
Unique in their own way,
It means someone's as different as
The night is to the day.

There's no one else – not anyone
Exactly just like you,
Since every child ever born
Was born to be brand new.

There is no one else in the world exactly like you.
What are your **UNIQUE** qualities?

I value the **V** and for reasons galore,
Since **values** are something in kids I adore.
And children who practice this very fine trait
Are often rewarded with wonderful fate.

A child with **values** just knows wrong from right
And would rather make up than continue a fight.
They're gentle with creatures who share our fine land
And helpful to others who need a warm hand.

They do the right thing, even though it could take
A little more effort than they might want to make.
They're sweet and they're caring and know that it's best
To try and be useful, instead of a pest.

So take it from me – since I know how this goes,
Your every deed matters and every act shows.
So, remember to always keep values in place
When making life choices you're certain to face.

Of all the **VALUES** you learned as we've traveled
through this book - which one do you **VALUE** most?

Now here's my sense of **W**,
The letter after "V"
And right before the edgy "X",
As you are next to see.

I made this word choice on a **whim**,
I didn't think it through.
I wanted to be **whimsical**,
It's such a kick to do!

This means you feel light inside,
You're open to new things
And freely acting on this sense,
No matter what it brings.

It means you do not figure out
What next you plan to do.
Instead you'll have an urge to act,
And quickly follow through.

So one day on a crazy **whim**,
Surprise yourself inside.
Try picking up a flute to play,
Or paint yourself a slide.

It doesn't really matter what
You choose to do that day,
Just try to let the **whimsical**
Come out in some fun way.

If you could just act on a **WHIM** and do something right in this moment, what would be an whimsical thing to do?

(You could also write about something you did on a whim in the past)

The **X** is sort of tricky,
Since there is no word around
That spells out any part of you,
At least not one I've found.

But did you know the **X** can be
A symbol all its own?
A sign that someone sends a kiss,
And **X** is how it's shown.

I wondered to myself one time
How **X** became a kiss.
But then I thought, "Who cares about
The 'how' or 'why' of this?"

It doesn't really matter how
This symbol came to be.
It only matters that I have
A kiss inside of me.

So when you see an **X** and **O**
Upon a page somewhere,
It means a kiss and hug is meant,
There's someone sending care.

Now, since we understand this sign
(I think we're right on track),
I'm blowing you a big fat **X**
And hope you'll "**X**" me back!

XOXOXOXOXOXOXOXOXOXO!

xoxo!

(Creating a collage of family, friends and pets could be fun here)

Y is **you**, and **you** are why
We made this alphabet.
Together we created art,
And now our book is set!

I loved our travels through each page,
While learning all about
The many roads that lead to **you**,
There's so much we found out!

We learned that both **your** head and heart
Together make a whole,
Combining all the things **you** are
Into a special soul.

So think about just who **you** are,
The many parts of **you**,
And how you'll use them in this life
In all **you're** yet to do.

It's up to **you** and no one else
That matters more to me,
So be **yourself** – all parts of **you** –
And be all **you** can be!

This page is all about **YOU**. Do whatever **YOU** want!

We've blazed a trail to the **Z**,
Our final letter, you can see.
So how about we make a deal
And finish with a little **zeal**?

Since **zeal** is a part of you
That adds some zip to all you do.
A zesty, zingy feeling where
A sense of thrill fills up the air!

Whenever you are full of spunk
(The opposite of *in a funk*)
And so pumped up you want to squeal,
You've tapped into this thing called **zeal**.

Myself – I feel **zeal** when
I realize where I have been,
And all the places yet to go
As I dance through this life I know.

So, live your life from A to Z,
Enjoying all you've come to be.
And thank you for this journey through
The ABCs of being you!

Will you sign our **ZEAL** Deal?

Let's Make a Deal with some Zeal!!

I, _____ hereby pledge the following:

Print name here

I will *APPRECIATE* the *BEAUTY* and *MAGIC* in the world.

I will be *NICE* to everyone (including me) and *CARE* always for the people, plants and animals living on our wonderful planet.

I will be *EAGER* about learning new things and *OPEN* to meeting new *FRIENDS*.

I will have a *PEP* in my step when I act on a *WHIM* to let my *SILLINESS* shine through.

I will be *QUIZZICAL* about what I don't know and be *GLAD* when I find the answers to my *KOOKY* questions.

I will *VALUE* my *UNIQUE* sense of *HUMOR* and use it to bring laughter into the world.

I will *TRUST* in myself and be *RESPONSIBLE* for being the best person I can be.

I will *DREAM* of my future and *IMAGINE* how much *JOY* there will be.

I will *LOVE* my life and all the people in it with total and complete *ZEAL!*

Please sign and accept here: _____

Dated: _____

X O X O X O X O